#1

HACK ATTACK

A TRIP TO WONDERLAND

magic
wagon

BY Jan Fields

visit us at www.abdopublishing.com

Published by Magic Wagon, a division of the ABDO Group,
PO Box 398166, Minneapolis, MN 55439. Copyright © 2013 by Abdo
Consulting Group, Inc. International copyrights reserved in all countries.

Calico Chapter Books™ is a trademark and logo of Magic Wagon.

Printed in the United States of America, North Mankato, Minnesota.
102012
012013
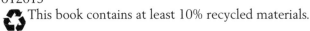

Written by Jan Fields
Cover illustration by Scott Altmann
Edited by Stephanie Hedlund and Grace Hansen
Cover and interior design by Neil Klinepier

Library of Congress Cataloging-in-Publication Data
Fields, Jan.
  Hack attack : a trip to Wonderland / by Jan Fields ; [illustrator, Scott
Altmann].
     p. cm. -- (Adventures in extreme reading ; bk. 1)
  Summary: Carter Lewis's Uncle Dan has invented a suit that creates a
virtual reality world so that the person experiences and interacts with
a book as if he were actually there--but when Carter and his cousin
Isabelle put on the suits they discover that a hacker is playing games
with them.
  ISBN 978-1-61641-919-6
1. Virtual reality--Juvenile fiction. 2. Computer hackers--Juvenile
fiction. 3. Books and reading--Juvenile fiction. 4. Inventors--Juvenile
fiction. 5. Inventions--Juvenile fiction. 6. Cousins--Juvenile fiction.
7. Uncles--Juvenile fiction. [1. Virtual reality--Fiction. 2. Computer
hackers--Fiction. 3. Books and reading--Fiction. 4. Inventors--Fiction. 5.
Inventions--Fiction. 6. Cousins--Fiction. 7. Uncles--Fiction.] I. Altmann,
Scott, ill. II. Title.
  PZ7.F479177Hac 2013
  813.6--dc23   2012023797

Table of Contents

A CODED MESSAGE

Carter hauled his backpack up on his shoulder as he trudged up the front steps. His mom stood right inside the front door juggling a portfolio and easel as she snagged her car keys from the rack beside the door.

"Hi, honey. How was school?" His mom reached up to brush his hair off his face only to have it fall right back. "We need to get you a haircut! I have to run or I'm going to be late for my painting class. Grab a snack. Dad's cooking tonight. I put your mail on your bed."

Carter blinked as his mom closed the door behind him. Sometimes these fast-forward conversations took a minute to sort out. Mail on his bed? Cool! He dashed up the stairs and dropped his backpack next to his desk with a thud. He snatched the postcard from his bed.

He knew it was from Uncle Dan before he even looked at the message. Dan Hunter collected weird postcards and sent them with his "secret" messages. The picture was usually some kind of hint.

This card showed two kids sitting a few inches away from a television, eyes intent on the screen. Behind them, two robots stood reading thick books. Carter wondered if his uncle was trying to teach robots to read, or maybe he was trying to hypnotize people by television. Uncle Dan worked on a lot of high-tech projects and some of them were supersecret things for the government.

Carter flipped the card over and noted the date first: 12/23/2009. At first glance it would look like his uncle was seriously behind in his mail, but Carter knew that the date was a clue to the code. Then he read the message:

You wouldn't believe the great new fishing rod I bought last week. I want to take you fishing so we can try it out. Our job will be to catch the biggest fish in the lake. We can top the giant catfish that we caught last year. My secret bait and this new rod are the key to success. I know the bait stinks. Fish don't think like us. That stuff is like giving the fish a call.

Carter knew that Uncle Dan hated fishing and would never ever buy a fishing pole. So that meant this was definitely a coded message. The date told him which words to underline. The string of numbers 12232009 meant that he needed to underline the first word in the first sentence, the second word in the second and third sentences, the third word in the fourth sentence, and so on. He had to skip the sixth and seventh sentences since they had zero code words.

When he was done, he knew the coded message was "You want job top secret call." He figured the first part was a question: "You want job?" The rest meant that the job was a secret and he should call his uncle.

Carter crammed his hand in his pocket to snag his cell phone. Then, he remembered it was dead because he'd dropped it in the toilet at school. You'd think phone companies would make those things waterproof.

He trotted downstairs to the phone in the kitchen to make the call. His uncle picked up on the first ring. "Speak," Uncle Dan said.

"I got your card," Carter said. "I'd love to . . . um . . . go fishing. I could really use a good fishing trip."

"Great," Uncle Dan said. "Come over tomorrow morning. We're taking Isabelle too."

Carter moaned at the click of his uncle hanging up. He couldn't think of too many things he'd enjoy less than working with his brainiac cousin.

"Maybe Dad will spring for one more phone," he muttered. "And I can pass on the Dizzy Izzy job."

Unfortunately, his parents did not respond well to his ruined cell phone.

"Carter Anthony Lewis," his mom said, "why exactly were you using your phone in the bathroom?"

"Because if I use it anywhere else, one of the teachers will take it away from me," he said. "And I needed to text Matt about something hysterical that happened in gym."

"Well, this time no one is laughing," his father said. "And no new cell phone unless you pay for it yourself."

The next morning, Carter was on his bike, heading toward his uncle's house. He hoped the job required him to work far away from his cousin. Carter could still hear his dad's patented responsibility lecture ringing in his ears as he turned into Uncle Dan's drive. He hopped off and wheeled the bike behind the little corral that held his uncle's garbage cans.

Uncle Dan insisted that they always keep their bikes from "prying eyes." Dizzy Izzy's blue and silver bike already leaned against the back of the corral.

As soon as Carter's knuckles hit the door, it flew open. Uncle Dan stood smiling at him. He was wearing a moldy orange life vest and a floppy hat decorated with fishing lures. "Come in," he bellowed cheerfully. "We're making new fishing lures."

"Sure," Carter yelled back. "I love fishing."

He followed his uncle through the door. Uncle Dan swept the hat off his head, revealing close-cropped brown hair in the exact same shade as Carter's longer mop. His uncle tossed the hat on the bench just inside the door. The life vest followed it.

"Where'd you get the hat?" Carter asked.

"Flea market. Don't touch it. It bites."

Carter started to suggest that maybe it shouldn't be left on a bench where people sit, but then he pictured Izzy plopping down on it and smiled. At that moment, Izzy peered over the first floor landing, her long straight hair hanging around her thin face, her mouth pinched. Carter thought she looked like she might be about to hurl over the railing, so he stepped carefully to one side.

"About time you got here!" she snapped.

Carter ignored her and followed Uncle Dan upstairs. "What's the job?" he asked.

"New project," Uncle Dan said. "It's going to revolutionize bookstores."

"Bookstores?" Carter echoed. "Your top secret project is something for bookstores? I thought it would be some cool government thing."

Uncle Dan laughed as he headed into the kitchen to grab sodas for everyone. Carter's uncle believed sugar and caffeine helped your brain work faster. He believed a lot of weird stuff. That's one of the things Carter liked about him. You never knew what to expect.

"Books are the seeds that grow worlds and topple governments. Come on down to the lab where I'll introduce you to the future," Uncle Dan said.

Uncle Dan's basement looked different

every time Carter visited, but you always saw computers—lots of computers and lots of monitors. Some of the screens showed views of the yard from cameras keeping watch over the whole property. But at least one monitor always had lines and lines of computer code. Today Uncle Dan walked by all of them and opened the door to his basement storage room.

Now the small room was almost empty except for two space suits hanging suspended from the ceiling from dozens of thin wires. They looked like giant space marionettes.

"You're making puppets?" Carter asked.

"Don't be a dope," Izzy whispered fiercely. Then, she turned to their uncle and sweetly asked, "Are you doing something for NASA?"

"No puppets and no NASA," Uncle Dan said, pushing his glasses up on his nose proudly. "You're looking at the new way to read a book!"

Carter and Izzy exchanged a look. Carter wondered if their uncle had finally lost it.

THE PLOT TWIST

"**H**ow do space suits help you read?" Carter asked.

He stepped into the small room and looked closer at the suits. The wires connecting them to the ceiling were a bit like bungy cords. "Hey, are these supposed to make you feel weightless?"

"Good guess," Uncle Dan said. Carter smirked at Izzy. "But wrong." His cousin smirked back. "These suits allow the 'reader' to have total immersion in a book. They are completely surrounded by it. It's virtual reality, but more real than anything you can imagine."

"I thought virtual reality was just done with goggles and sometimes gloves," Izzy said. "Why do you need a whole suit?"

"Goggles just let you see," Uncle Dan explained. "These suits let you do everything. You can walk, smell, touch, and hear. If you trudge through the snow, the suit will make your feet cold. If you trek through a jungle, you'll smell the flowers and feel the heat. If you're standing on the deck of a ship, you'll feel the spray of the water and smell the fish guts."

"Wow," Carter said softly.

"If someone grabs you in the story," Uncle Dan went on, "the suit will tighten on your arm in just that spot. You'll feel them grab you. You feel everything."

"Sounds dangerous," Izzy said, folding her arms over her chest.

"Nope, it's totally safe."

Izzy continued to look doubtful and Uncle Dan grinned. "Okay, I had some trouble with early prototypes causing vomiting and a few bruises. Nothing serious though."

Izzy narrowed her eyes and pointed accusingly at her uncle. "You're hiring us to test the suits because we're family. That way you won't get sued if we puke."

"No, no." Uncle Dan held up a hand in protest, and then he dropped it. "Okay, yes. But it's also a fantastic experience, and I'm willing to pay."

"I'll do it," Carter said. He needed the money. Then he paused. "Did you clean the puke out of the suits?"

"Sure, sure." Uncle Dan rubbed his hands together excitedly. "So you guys want to try it? The suits are easy to step into and they'll adjust for your difference in size automatically." He showed them how the suits opened at the back and they both scrambled inside.

The inside of the suit was completely dark, and Carter suspected this would not be fun if you were claustrophobic. Luckily, he wasn't. Much.

"Are we going to start soon?" he asked, wincing at the embarrassing squeak in his voice.

"Firing up." Uncle Dan spoke right in Carter's ear, as if his uncle had leaned close to him and whispered in the total darkness. It was a spooky feeling. Carter waited for some kind of computer sounds, but all he heard was his uncle. "Okay, running some diagnostics. Do you see anything?"

Carter looked around. He just saw blackness. He started to say so when he spotted a light dimly in the distance. "I see a light far away."

"Me too," Izzy's voice spoke into his other ear. Carter automatically turned toward her. He realized he could see his cousin a little in the dim light. But she wasn't in a suit. She just looked normal.

"When did you take the suit off?" Carter asked.

"I didn't," Izzy answered, and Carter could see her lips move. "But I see you, and you're not in a suit."

"The program renders you in the virtual reality, so you won't see a suit," Uncle Dan said. "If you were in a real book, you'd be wearing clothes to suit the story."

"Cool," Izzy said.

Carter held his hand in front of his face and saw bare fingers even though he knew he was wearing the suit. It was freaky. Then he noticed the light had come a lot closer. He recognized that it was the glow of a lantern being carried by a little kid.

The kid was younger than Isabelle and Carter. He held the lantern up to stare at them. "Are you ghosts?" the boy asked.

"No," Carter said. "Are you?"

The little boy laughed.

"Okay," Uncle Dan interrupted. "Clearly you see my test character, Carter. Do you see it too, Izzy?"

"I sure do," Izzy said. "It's a little boy with a lantern. He looks about seven and is wearing Victorian clothes."

"Show off," Carter muttered.

"I need to be going," the little boy said. "Would you like my lantern?"

"Should I take it, Uncle Dan?" Carter asked.

"Yes."

Carter took the lantern from the boy. He could feel the weight of it as the slightly rough wire handle pressed into his hand. He held it up closer to his face and blinked at the brightness of the light. He could feel the warmth coming off it.

"I can feel it," he whispered.

"Let me try," Izzy demanded. Carter reluctantly handed her the lamp. She held a hand close to the lantern chimney and grinned. "That's fantastic."

"Okay, do either of you feel queasy?" Uncle Dan asked. "Light-headed? Does anything hurt?"

"No," they said in unison.

"Good! I'm going to start up a book then. Get ready, this should be amazing."

Suddenly the space around Carter burst with light, sound, and smell. He could feel an uneven dirt road under his feet and smell the piles of horse poop that dotted the road ahead.

He glanced at Izzy and saw she was wearing a long gown that presently dragged dangerously close to one steaming pile. Carter smiled.

"We're on a road," Izzy said as she looked around. "It's midmorning."

"And this road apparently gets a lot of horse traffic," Carter added. "It stinks."

"Fantastic," Uncle Dan said. "But you don't feel like puking?"

"No," Carter said. "I'm good."

"I see someone coming," Izzy said, shading her eyes against the bright morning sun. "He's on a yellow horse."

Carter watched as the horse plodded closer. The animal was incredibly skinny with sores on its legs. It walked with its head hung as if always hoping to run across a stray snack.

The rider was only a few years older than Carter with a long face and a heavy jaw. He wore a faded tunic and a beret with a feather. He bounced a bit awkwardly in the saddle as the horse walked. A sword strapped into a shoulder belt slapped against him with each uneven step the old horse took.

"I know who this is," Izzy said with a grin.

"Who?"

"It's d'Artagnan," she said. "From *The Three Musketeers*!"

"That's a musketeer?" Carter asked, laughing. "I didn't picture them riding something that looked like a cartoon horse!"

"Be careful, Carter," Uncle Dan said. "D'Artagnan was touchy about his horse."

"He should be," Carter said, still laughing.

As the old yellow horse grew close, the young man glared down at them. "Are you laughing at something?" he asked sharply.

"No, sir," Izzy said sweetly. "We were merely enjoying a lovely day."

D'Artagnan's eyes narrowed as he stared at her. Then he turned to Carter. "And you?" he asked.

"Well," Carter said, "maybe I was laughing a little, but she started it. If you want to run her through with your sword, that's cool with me."

"Carter!" his cousin snapped.

"I am no barbarian who assaults women," d'Artagnan said, swinging his leg over the horse and hopping down. "I hold you responsible. En garde!" D'Artagnan pulled out his sword as Carter stepped back.

"Chill, dude. One for all and all for one, remember?" Suddenly, Carter felt something in his right hand. He glanced down to find a sword. "Whoa, cool, a sword!"

"Hold on," Uncle Dan's voice said. "A what?"

"It's okay," Carter said, swishing the blade through the air. "I've always wanted to try sword fighting. This could be fun."

"You should not have a sword," his uncle practically shouted in his ear.

"Watch out," Izzy said as she looked at d'Artagnan's fierce glare. "Those things look sharp. And d'Artagnan is an amazing swordsman."

D'Artagnan looked sharply at Izzy. "How do

you know my name?"

She shrugged. "Lucky guess?"

D'Artagnan's blade sliced the air with a whistle as he turned back toward Carter. "Tell me how you know my name, and perhaps I will let you live."

Carter held up his sword and shouted, "I am not afraid of you! I will tell you nothing!" He rushed at d'Artagnan, flailing wildly with his sword.

The tip of the young man's sword caught Carter's blade near the hilt and flicked it out of his hand. Then d'Artagnan stalked closer, his sword raised.

"Okay," Carter said, raising his hands. "I give up. Really, I'll tell you anything you want."

D'Artagnan leaned so close that Carter could smell sausage and tooth decay on his breath.

"Hey," Carter yelped as the angry young man grabbed his arm tightly. Then he felt a sharp poke in his side from d'Artagnan's sword. "Ow!"

"The cat," d'Artagnan whispered in a flat,

creepy voice. "The cat blows in on thunder cloud feet."

"That's it!" Carter heard his uncle's voice in his ears and suddenly everything went dark. The pressure of d'Artagnan's fingers disappeared from Carter's arm.

"Get out of the suits now!" Uncle Dan ordered. "Something is seriously wrong."

A CAT IN THE FOG

Carter felt the suit open behind him and welcomed the chance to step out. He ran his hand over his side and sighed with relief when he didn't find any blood.

"What went wrong?" he asked his uncle.

"Right offhand," his cousin said as she clambered out of her suit, "I'd guess d'Artagnan isn't supposed to attack players or try to quote poetry by Carl Sandburg."

"Huh?" Carter asked. He hated it when Isabelle made him feel stupid, which was most of the time. "What are you talking about?"

"That line about the cat feet," she said. "It's a misquote from a poem."

"The fog comes on little cat feet," Uncle Dan said as he headed back to his row of computers and peered at the screen where code scrolled continuously. "That's the real line. And it doesn't belong in *The Three Musketeers*."

"How did it get in there?" Carter asked.

His uncle looked up at him, his face tense. "There's only one way I can think of. I've been hacked. Someone got into the program and messed with the book. The question is, is it just this book or all the books?"

"Wouldn't the bigger question be who?" Carter asked. "Or why?"

"I know why," Uncle Dan muttered. He leaned so close to the monitor that Carter expected his nose to touch. "As for who, the number of hackers who have the skills to get into my system is small, but I've been out of that community for a while. I don't know all the players."

Carter stepped closer to Izzy and whispered, "Do you know why someone would hack the system?"

Izzy shoved her hair behind her ears and gave Carter her "you're stupid" look. Then she said, "Some kind of industrial sabotage probably. Someone wants to ruin Uncle Dan's chances of perfecting and selling this system, probably so they can sell their own. This thing is worth millions."

"Oh," Carter said. "But why add poetry?"

Uncle Dan froze and looked up at Carter. "You know, that's a good question. Why not make the character spout gibberish? Why not just have the program crash?"

"Maybe a program crash was too obvious. The hacker didn't want you to be able to fix the problem too soon," Izzy said.

"Maybe." Their uncle nodded slightly. "But that doesn't explain the poetry." Then a slow smile came over his face.

Carter felt totally lost. He had dreams like this, where you walk into a room and everyone acts like they know something you don't. He looked down to make sure he was wearing pants—okay, good, he wasn't dreaming. Those dreams always ended up with him standing around in his underwear.

"What are you thinking?" Izzy asked.

"I'm thinking this hacker likes playing games. The poetry is some kind of clue," Uncle Dan said. "Hackers have big, big egos. They like to imagine they're smarter than everyone else. Secretly they want the credit for the mischief they make. I'm thinking the line is a clue to who did this."

Uncle Dan looked at Carter. "Do you remember exactly what d'Artagnan said?"

Carter nodded. "'The cat. The cat blows in on thunder cloud feet.' That's sort of the opposite of the real line, right?"

"So maybe the hacker is called The Cat," Izzy suggested.

"Possibly, but I doubt it's that easy. I think we're going to have to look for other things that don't fit in the story," Uncle Dan said.

"Can't you just check the computer code?"

Isabelle asked.

Uncle Dan turned to the screen that was presently scrolling code. "Sure, I could run all the code against the backups that have been in a secure, non-networked computer. That would let me fix the books, but it wouldn't show me what the code does. I think we're going to need to isolate the changed code and look at the differences from inside the program," he said. "Once we find out what the change does, I can fix it. But more importantly, we can see if there is a pattern in the clues."

"So we need to suit up again?" Carter asked. He was eager to get back into the virtual world and see what else the program could do. Would he have more sword fights? Ride horses? Things had just started to get interesting when they left last time.

"Not today," Uncle Dan said. "I want to go through the code a little. I don't want to put you guys in there if these changes are dangerous."

Carter waved a hand. "I'm not afraid to

puke. And d'Artagnan didn't scare me. I could have taken him if you hadn't shut down the program."

Isabelle laughed. "Yeah, I could tell you were terrifying him with your swordsmanship."

Uncle Dan held up a hand to stop the squabbles and looked at them seriously. "The bottom line is that you don't get back in the suits until I'm convinced the hacks are harmless. These suits could do much worse than you've seen so far. Much, much worse."

"Way to creep a guy out," Carter muttered.

Then his uncle smiled and patted him on the back. "Just let me check them out. Come back in the morning. I'll pay you for today before you go."

Before Carter knew it, he had money in his pocket and he was being shoved out the front door along with his cousin.

"Are you coming back tomorrow?" Izzy asked.

"Wouldn't miss it," Carter replied.

The next morning, Carter got to Uncle Dan's house so early that the sun was still a rosy glow on the clouds. He smiled when he parked his bike and saw that he'd beat Izzy. Trotting up the front walk, he spotted a postcard tacked to the door. He grabbed it and found Uncle Dan's small, precise handwriting crammed in the message spot.

12/18/2010

Gone for a few days to feel out some companies about video game project. Staying underground so much was making me twitchy. To earn some extra money, you and Isabelle can keep testing the game system. Isabelle can run the computers; Carter can catch some adventures. Play "Hacker" as much as you like, the game cartridge is in the box. Take notes and let me know what you think. Careful notes will help me fix any issues now before we go to market. See ya soon.

Carter worked out the message in his head: "Gone underground to catch Hacker. Careful!" He wondered if the rest of the message was telling them to keep looking for clues or if it was just silly like the fishing message on the first card. He decided to keep looking for clues.

Carter knelt behind a tall shrub and pulled the spare key out of the downspout. Uncle Dan kept it inside a realistic and disgusting rubber slug. He let himself in, snagged a soda from the fridge, and waited for Izzy. When the doorbell rang, he let his cousin in and showed her the card their uncle had left.

She nodded as she decoded it in her head. "So we're supposed to look for clues in the book program while Uncle Dan's away?"

"I wasn't sure," Carter said. "The note looks like it, but the coded part doesn't say."

"We should check downstairs, there may be more instructions there."

The cousins trotted down the stairs. They found the basement door locked and a small speaker mounted next to the door. Uncle Dan's voice came from the speaker as they approached, "Before the day, after the night, when darkness ends, what is the light?"

Izzy frowned, thinking. Then she looked at Carter and shrugged. Suddenly the voice spoke again, "This system will lock down in thirty seconds. Before the day, after the night, when darkness ends, what is the light?"

Carter thought frantically. What comes before day? Was it a word puzzle? When darkness ends, the light is the sun and sun comes before day in Sunday.

"Sun," he said.

"Password denied," Dan's voice calmly answered. "Lockdown in ten seconds."

What comes before day but after night? "Morning!" Carter shouted.

"Password accepted," Uncle Dan said. When Carter tried the knob again, it opened easily. The cousins hurried into the room, switching on the lights. Izzy headed straight to the computer table. She flipped through the spiral-bound log Uncle Dan always kept when he was working on a project.

"It looks like he compared the code in *The Three Musketeers* to the original and that one piece of poetry was the only abnormality," she said. "I think we need to start with a different book."

"What books do we have to choose from?" Carter asked.

"A lot," Izzy said as she tapped keys and called up a list.

Carter scanned the list and wrinkled his nose. "These are all really old books. Why didn't he do anything new and cool?"

"Copyright," she said absently, leaning closer to the monitor.

"Who's right?" Carter asked.

Isabelle sighed and spun to face him. "Copyright. It just means you don't need to pay to use really old stuff. Now what book should we use?"

Carter shrugged. "It doesn't matter. You pick."

Izzy broke into a grin. "Okay. Suit up, cousin."

Carter headed for the suit room with the sinking feeling that he may have just made a really big mistake.

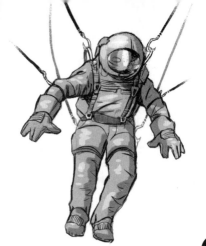

Down the Rabbit Hole

Carter climbed into the suit and felt a nervous twitch in his stomach as Izzy closed up the back. He really didn't like all this darkness. Then he heard her voice in his ear, "Do you hear me?"

"Yeah," he said. "Let's do it."

The dark lay against him for another few seconds, then he was dazzled by bright sunlight. Carter looked around a small, grassy field dotted with trees. Suddenly, a white rabbit in a checkered vest rushed by, running along on its back legs. A moment later a young girl followed. He recognized the rabbit.

"Oh, come on, Izzy," he moaned. *"Alice in Wonderland?"*

His cousin giggled in his ear. "Think of it as an adventure. Besides, I had to pick a book I've read so we'll know if something was changed."

"Right." Carter dashed off after the pair as they raced toward a hedge. Then both rabbit and girl bent low and disappeared into a row of tall bushes. Carter knew enough about *Alice in Wonderland* to remember that she fell into a hole somewhere along here. He didn't intend to do the same.

He stepped closer to the hedge cautiously and spotted a tunnel, partly hidden by the shade of the bushes. The tunnel sloped downward gradually. Carter crouched down and half crawled in.

"This tunnel needs a higher ceiling," he complained. "I'm a lot taller than Alice."

"I don't think it should be a problem for long," Izzy said.

Carter shuffled on until he reached a spot where the floor simply seemed to fall away. He peered down into the hole, but all he could see was an endless drop. "That's one deep hole," he whispered.

"Jump in," Izzy said.

"I can't see the bottom!"

"It should be fine. It doesn't hurt Alice in the book," Izzy said.

"Yeah, but that was before the program was hacked," he said. "Who knows how far I could fall now?"

"Don't be a baby."

Carter gritted his teeth. He wondered how brave she'd be if she were standing here. Then he took a deep breath and jumped. He felt as if he were falling in slow motion. For a moment, he wondered if he really might puke. But then his stomach settled and he looked around as he fell.

The walls of the shaft held cubbies and shelves filled with all kinds of things. He wondered if any of the stuff could be clues.

"Write this down," he told Izzy. Then he snatched things off shelves, named them, and then deposited each on the next empty shelf. "Oil lamp, tea pot with a lightning bolt painted on the side, bent spoon, book." He held the book close to his face in the gloom of the tunnel. "The title is *The Tornado of Oz*."

"That's not the right title," Izzy said.

"Should be 'wizard' instead of 'tornado,' right?" Carter said.

"Well, actually," Izzy said in her know-it-all voice, "there is a whole series of Oz books, but none have that title."

"So, it's a clue?"

"Maybe," Izzy said.

'There was only one clue in the first book," Carter said. "So if this is the clue, I should come on out."

"We can't be sure," Isabelle answered. "Stay a little longer."

Carter frowned. He suspected his cousin was just tormenting him. He picked up a few more things—a ship in a bottle, a mostly empty jar of orange jelly, a floppy stuffed cat.

"Hey, I've got a stuffed cat here," he said. "That's two cats in two books. Do you think it's a clue?"

"I'll write it down," she answered.

Carter tossed the cat on the next shelf. It was the last shelf he passed before he hit bottom, landing in a pile of sticks and leaves. He stood and dusted himself off. A long hallway with doors on each side stretched ahead of him. He ran to door after door, but they were all locked.

"I'm in a hallway of locked doors," he said.

"That's normal," Izzy answered. "Keep going."

"Okay, I see a glass table with a little key on it and a bottle that says 'Drink Me!'," he said. "And there's a puddle on the floor."

"Okay, stand in the puddle and drink the stuff in the bottle," Izzy ordered.

"Are you sure?" Carter stepped into the puddle and uncorked the bottle.

"I read the book," she said. "Drink it! You can swim."

Carter was already swallowing when he

thought to wonder what swimming had to do with anything. That's when the water started to rise around him. Carter looked around and saw the table looming larger and larger nearby. He was shrinking!

He didn't stop shrinking until he had to tread water. That's when he spotted Alice swimming briskly behind a giant mouse.

"This place is weird," he muttered as he set off after them.

"Curiouser and curiouser," Izzy said.

"Huh?"

"I'm quoting," Izzy grumbled. "You're fine. Swimming is in the book."

As he swam, he noticed more and more animals in the water. They were all heading in the same direction, so he swam along. With his longer arms and stronger swimming, he could have passed Alice, but he slowed to follow her instead.

Finally, they all scrambled out of the water and onto a dry riverbank, which made no sense at all since the puddle had been on a floor of a hall.

"This book is screwed up," Carter complained.

"Well," Izzy answered. "It is supposed to be like a dream."

Suddenly Alice turned to look at him, her long hair dripping onto her sodden dress. "And who are you?"

"Carter," he said.

"Mr. Carter," she said politely, "do you know what we should do to get dry?"

"I shall tell a very dry story," the mouse suggested.

"I don't think that will help," Alice answered before turning to look up at Carter again.

"What should we do to get dry?" Carter whispered for Izzy.

"I think you're supposed to run around," Izzy said.

"We should run around," Carter said to Alice. She curtsied in thanks.

"But my story is very dry," the mouse

squeaked, punctuating his remark with a sneeze.

"Energetic measures do seem to be in order," suggested a fat bird with a huge, cartoonish beak.

"Speak English," demanded a young eagle who glared at the other bird. The young eagle towered over Carter and looked more than a little scary with his sharp eyes and even sharper beak.

"We should run around," Carter suggested again.

"But my story," the mouse insisted, then he began to speak in an odd flat voice. "The Earl of Northumbria found the weather quite dry. As dry as dust. As dry as desert sand. But the rains came. And the hail. And the wicked, wicked winds. And the sleet."

"What is that mouse going on about?" Izzy asked.

"The weather," Carter answered.

"The weather!" shouted all the creatures

together, turning to glare at Carter. They began to speak in robotic unison as they walked closer to him. "The storm is fierce. The storm is rough. The storm is out of control."

"Okay, I don't think this is in the book," Carter said, backing away as the creatures continued to press toward him.

Suddenly something grabbed his hand. It was Alice. "You wouldn't run away, would you, Mr. Carter?" she asked in her soft, little girl voice. Carter swallowed a lump in his throat as he looked down at her. She smiled back and something about her smile made his stomach knot up. It was a bit too wide and toothy, and she held it entirely too long.

"This is extremely creeptastic," he said, trying to pull his hand loose as her fingers gripped tighter and tighter. "I think we should hop out of this book."

"I'm trying," Izzy said. "The hacker has changed the shut down protocols. Give me a minute."

Carter continued to back away from the slowly advancing animals as they muttered about the weather. Since Alice wouldn't let go, he just pulled her along with him.

"Anytime now, Izzy," he whispered.

"Still trying." Her voice sounded high and thin.

Suddenly, Carter backed into something. He whirled around, still dragging Alice along. The White Rabbit stood almost nose to nose with him. It leaned close and said, "The queen won't like this weather, and you know what she'll do."

The rabbit drew his paw across the front of his throat. "Off with your head."

THE MAD TEA PARTY

"**I**zzy!" Carter shouted as he ducked around the scary rabbit and dragged Alice into a small forest beyond. "I'm so ready to get out of here."

"I'm still working on it," she said. "I think I can build in a backdoor to get you out. You'll just need to get to . . ."

"Get to where?" he yelled, but she didn't answer. "Izzy?"

"I'm not Izzy," Alice said as she stumbled along behind him. "Why do you keep calling me Izzy?"

"I'm not calling you Izzy," Carter said as he scrambled down a small slope and landed on a path. "I was talking to my cousin."

"Is she invisible?" Alice asked.

"Something like that," Carter said. He looked up and down the path. Both ways eventually twisted into the trees without giving any hint of where they might end up.

"Do you know which way to go?" Carter asked.

"We could ask the cat," Alice said, pointing to a nearby tree branch where a very large cat sat grinning from ear to ear. The cat stretched, showing off long, curved claws that looked entirely too sharp in Carter's opinion.

"Does it talk?" he asked.

"It does," said the cat.

"Oh, good," Carter said. "Do you know which way we should go?"

"That depends a good deal on where you want to get to," the cat said. It grinned even bigger. Carter blinked at how many pointed teeth the thing had. It looked like a cartoon shark.

"What happens if we go that way?" he asked, pointing uphill on the trail.

"The Mad Hatter's house lies that way.

Though you can get to the March Hare's house as well. It depends upon which way you go when the path splits," the cat said. "But I cannot say what will actually happen if you go to either place. They're both quite mad."

"Terrific. How about that way?" Carter pointed the opposite direction.

"The duchess lives that way," the cat said. "She has a terrible temper and her cook will certainly throw pepper and cutlery. How good are you at ducking and weaving?"

"I'm not sure. What exactly is cutlery?" Carter echoed.

"Knives," Alice chimed in helpfully.

"The cook throws knives? Okay, then we go visit the crazy folks," Carter said, dragging Alice up the hill. Suddenly he stopped. "Could you let go of my hand?"

Alice looked down at their hands in surprise. "I don't believe I can," she whispered.

"Of course not," Carter muttered. He stomped along with the girl clinging tightly to his hand, trotting to keep up. As soon as they reached the top of the hill, they spotted the strangest house Carter had ever seen. The chimneys were shaped like ears and the roof was thatched with fur.

"Well, the path never divided, but my guess is that is the March Hare's house."

"It's very large," Alice said.

"With my luck," Carter grumbled, "he's a giant rabbit."

There was a long formal table set out under a tree in front of the house. At one end of the table, the March Hare and the Mad Hatter sat together having tea. Between them, a dormouse slumped, fast asleep. The hatter and the hare were using the dormouse as a cushion. They were resting their elbows on it and talking over its head.

"I don't think I would like being a cushion," Alice whispered to Carter.

He nodded as they walked closer. The table was very long with chairs all along the sides. A delicate china cup and saucer and a small plate of toast sat before each chair.

The Mad Hatter looked sharply at Carter and flapped his hand. "No room. Go along now. We have no room!"

"No room," the March Hare echoed. "No room."

"No, no, no," muttered the sleepy mouse.

"There's *plenty* of room!" Alice insisted. She sat down in a large armchair at the opposite end of the table, dragging Carter along with her this time. He took a seat beside her. He hoped she would need both hands for the tea and let go of him. He was getting really tired of holding hands.

The Mad Hatter peered at Carter. "Your hair wants cutting."

"That's what my mom tells me."

The Hatter sat up very tall and smiled. "She must be a woman of amazing intellect. Since you are her son, perhaps you know . . ." He leaned as far across the table as he could reach and pointed a butter knife at Carter. "Why is a raven like a lightning flash?"

Lightning? Carter wondered if this was another clue. He suddenly wished very hard that he could talk to his cousin. Still, this sounded like a riddle and he was good at riddles.

"Well," the March Hare said, "do you think you can find out the answer to that?"

Carter held up his hand. "Give me a minute!"

"A minute!" The Hatter pulled a huge watch from his pocket and began beating it against the tabletop. "Tick, tock. Time is running out! And I feel a storm coming!"

"A powerful storm," the March Hare added.

"Storm! Storm!" the dormouse squeaked.

Alice began to sway back and forth in her seat and sing in a high voice. "Twinkle, twinkle, lightning bolt! Come and strike this silly dolt! Up above the world so high! I control you from the sky!"

"Up above the world so high!" echoed the Mad Hatter.

"Solve the clues before you die," the March Hare sang, his voice hollow.

Die? Carter looked sharply at the March Hare. His long, rabbity teeth had grown past his chin and turned steel gray. Carter suspected he was about to wear out his welcome at this particular party.

The Mad Hatter was slashing his butter knife through the air like a sword. As Carter watched, the knife grew longer and sharper.

"It would please the queen, I think," the Hatter said, rising slowly to his feet, "if I cut off your head. Perhaps she'll invite me to the palace." The Hatter swished the knife through the air and neatly shaved a stripe of fur from the back of the dormouse.

Carter stood up, pulling Alice to her feet. "Great party, guys, but we should be going."

"Stay, stay," the March Hare said, sparks flying from his new steel teeth as he spoke. "It's time to play!"

"Izzy!" Carter yelled. "This would be a great

time to get me out of here."

Since he didn't hear any reply, he figured he better get himself out of there. Carter spun and ran again, pulling Alice along behind him. He heard the Hatter and March Hare whooping as they scrambled around the table after them.

Carter risked one glance back. The Hatter was waving his butter-knife sword as he trotted along. Then the March Hare leapfrogged over the Hatter and galloped closer, sparks flying as it gnashed its long teeth.

A CHANGE OF ALICE

Carter half ran, half stumbled along the trail. Dragging Alice slowed him up. More than once, panic made him pull the little girl off her feet, and he had to stop and wait for her to get up again.

They had left the slower Mad Hatter behind. But each time they had to stop, Carter saw the March Hare behind them, giggling and twitching as he hopped along. Sometimes the hare would hop entirely off the trail and slash his steel teeth at the trees. At one point, the March Hare paused and looked directly into Carter's eyes. It pointedly leaned over and bit a thick sapling in two.

"This book," Carter panted as Alice scrambled back to her feet for the fourth time, "is really not appropriate for children."

"Fun is fun," the March Hare shouted, his voice lispy now from his overly long teeth. "The game is won. Even if you run and run."

Carter didn't like the sound of that at all. The March Hare lowered his head and leaped forward, halving the distance between them on the narrow trail. The thing would be on them in a second. Carter looked around for a weapon. He grabbed a stick with his free hand as he hauled Alice around behind him.

"Fighting would be a lot easier if you'd let go of my hand!" he yelled. And at that instant, the grip of Alice's hand vanished. Carter didn't waste time glancing back at her. He grabbed his stick with both hands and hoped the March Hare didn't turn it into toothpicks at the first snap.

The March Hare grinned as he gathered himself for a huge leap. Just then, a girl with long, blonde hair and a white apron stepped from behind a tree. She smacked the March

Hare's metal teeth with a baseball bat. The bat broke as the teeth sheered off at the roots. Then the March Hare tumbled backward and lay sprawled on the trail.

The girl turned to Carter and he gasped, "Isabelle?"

"No time to chat now, cousin," she said. "Run!"

So he ran with Izzy thundering along behind him. They raced past the point on the trail where Carter had seen the talking cat and finally staggered to a stop, panting in a small clearing just beyond.

"That crazy rabbit doesn't seem to be following us," he gasped. He bent over with his hands on his knees to catch his breath.

"It might be limited to its own area," Izzy panted back.

They focused on breathing in relative silence for a moment. Then Carter stood up and asked, "What are you doing here?"

"I think the code I inserted in the program to

let you out of the book accidentally shut down communications somehow," Izzy said. When Carter opened his mouth to protest, she held up her hand. "You're only allowed to complain if you could do better.

"Anyway, I found a way out of the program. It should shut the book down, but you have to be in the right spot and do the right thing to trigger it. Since I couldn't talk to you from the outside, I changed the program to let me take Alice's place." She looked down at the long dress and stockings in disgust. "I didn't have time to change her costuming."

"Is there a baseball bat in *Alice in Wonderland?*" Carter asked.

"No, I added that," she said. "The program wouldn't let me put in anything more deadly. It gives the crazy hare steel teeth, but it won't let me have anything tougher than a baseball bat. Which is now broken, so we should probably try to avoid any more killer characters."

"I second that vote," Carter said. He pointed

down the trail. "The cat said that trail led to the Duchess's house. I don't suppose you put the backdoor there?"

Izzy shook her head. "It's at the Queen's palace. That's as close as I could get it."

Carter looked around the woods. "How do we get there from here?" he wondered out loud.

Izzy shrugged. "In the real book, the cat and the caterpillar both gave directions. Or if we find the White Rabbit, we could follow him. He ends up at the palace."

"I would rather stay away from rabbits," Carter said. He turned and continued on the trail. "Since we don't want to revisit the hare, I guess we should go look for the caterpillar. I definitely don't want to revisit the cat. I'm telling you, his teeth and claws aren't exactly relaxing to be around."

"Wait, we might not need either one. Do you know the way back to the hall?" Izzy asked. "There's a door to the palace garden in the hall."

Carter thought for a moment. "Yeah, we

need to leave the trail up where I talked to the cat last time." He glanced nervously back the way they had come. "That way."

"Great." Izzy set off up the hill.

Carter figured it was easier to be brave if you had only just gotten here. The terror needed time to grow on you, he decided. He trudged along behind her, watching the shadowy woods for any vicious wildlife.

"This must be it," Izzy said. She stopped so suddenly that Carter almost knocked her down.

"All the woods look alike," he said. "How do you know this is the spot?"

"Because the Cheshire Cat is right there." Izzy pointed.

The Cheshire Cat's smile hung in the air above a branch. Since that's the only part of the cat visible, it was easy to miss.

"Could you tell us how to get back to the hall?" Carter asked.

"The hall?" the cat repeated as he slowly grew more and more visible. First his very green eyes, then his nose, then his head hung in space for a while. Carter found it amazingly creepy. "Which hall? Town hall? Hall of mirrors?"

"The hall of doors," Carter said.

"The one with the door to the Queen's garden," Izzy said.

The cat tilted his head and gazed at Isabelle for a moment. "You look different," he said. "You are definitely taller. Have you been eating a mushroom?"

"Something like that," Izzy answered.

"You can get to the hall through the Duchess's cellar," the cat said. "Or the White Rabbit's linen closet or you can close your eyes and walk that way." He pointed with his long tail, which had appeared just for that purpose. "Simply walk until you feel floor under your feet."

"Wouldn't we walk into trees?" Carter asked.

"I wouldn't," the cat replied.

"We should try the walking," Isabelle said. "It's closest and doesn't require interacting with any more characters. You seem to have annoyed a lot of them."

"That was not my fault," Carter insisted, but he turned toward the woods.

"As much as I hate suggesting this," Isabelle said, making a pinched face. "We should hold hands so we don't get separated with our eyes closed."

She held out her hand. Carter took it and managed not to shudder. He thought shuddering might be rude in light of her saving his life from the crazy hare.

They closed their eyes and began walking forward. Carter expected to feel the rough smack of a tree against him at any moment, but none came. He could feel the leaves and roots under his feet as he shuffled forward slowly. He could even smell the earthy scent of decaying leaves and pine sap.

Then with the next small step, he felt smooth, hard floor.

"I think we made it," he whispered. He opened his eyes to find they were definitely back in the long hall of huge doors. He dropped Isabelle's hand and they looked around.

"Opening one of these doors is going to take some work," he said. He stretched as tall as he could and barely brushed his fingers against the nearest doorknob. "Do you know which door we want? We'll be here forever if we have to do this by trial and error."

Isabelle shook her head. "When we find the right door, it should be just the right size for us." Her brow wrinkled as she tried to remember. "Also, I think it's behind a curtain."

They strode forward and soon found a blue curtain, looking curiously out of place, hanging on the wall. They pulled it back and discovered an arched door that was only slightly shorter than Carter. The door had no handle, but right in the middle was an oversized lock with a huge keyhole. He pushed against the door and found it locked, then he glanced at Isabelle.

"The key is on the glass table," she said.

They continued down the hall to what looked

like a tall ice sculpture, but was really the legs of a table. When Carter looked up, he saw a glass tabletop far above them. It was like looking up at a skyscraper. What were they going to do now?

A GLASSY CLIMB

Carter turned to his cousin. "That key is a long way up there," he said. "How did Alice reach that?"

"Mushroom," Izzy said as she looked over the table legs. "She had pieces of the mushroom where the caterpillar sat. One piece made you tall and the other made you shrink. We don't have any of that."

"We have to go find a caterpillar?" Carter asked. "Shouldn't you have told me that when we were in the woods?"

Isabelle shook her head. "I would rather not go back to interacting with the characters until we have to. They seem to be unusually aggressive."

"Yeah, that's how I would describe them,"

Carter said, shaking his head. "Or killer crazy. So, how do we get the key way up there? Or do you have lock-picking skills I don't know about?"

"We climb," Izzy said. She stepped closer to the nearest leg. "Look how ornate this thing is. There are tons of hand- and footholds. We've both been rock climbing. We can do this."

Carter walked to the nearest table leg. It was made to look like a flowering vine wrapped around a clear glass core. Izzy was right about the number of handholds and footholds, though the smooth glass would make for tricky climbing.

"We had safety equipment when we went rock climbing," Carter said. He peered up into the distance to see how the legs were attached to the tabletop. It wouldn't help much to climb it if all they could do was get to the top of a leg and hang there. He saw that near the top, the legs slowly spread out until they were nearly horizontal just before joining to the edge of the tabletop.

"Remember, we aren't really going to be climbing anything," Isabelle said. "We're in funky space suits in Uncle Dan's basement. If we fall, we're not really plummeting to our deaths. How much can it hurt?"

Carter looked at her nervously. That just sounded like begging for trouble to him. He wasn't sure how much these suits could hurt, but he suspected the answer was a lot. "Okay, but why do we both need to climb?"

"Because it looks like you might need to boost me over the edge of the tabletop once we get that high. I can't tell for sure, but that last bit is going to be the trickiest part. I think we should both be there when we reach that part."

Looking up, Carter realized she was right. "Okay," he said as he walked over to the closest leg. "Let's do it."

He began the climb quickly, but the smooth glass soon had him slowing down for safety. The hand- and footholds were plentiful but slippery. Izzy climbed after him. Before he'd gotten halfway, his arms were shaking from the strain of the climb. He paused and leaned in close to the leg, taking his weight off his hands. He shook out his arms, one and then the other, wiping his palms on his pants to keep them dry. Sweaty hands could kill on this climb.

"Are you stuck?" Izzy's voice called up.

"Just resting," Carter said. He started up again. The climb went from exciting and scary to tiring and scary. In the last bit, it eased on over into exhausting. He couldn't even pull up enough energy to be scared. Then he reached the point where the legs gently curved outward. He carefully climbed around the leg and scrambled across the gentle curve. When it was nearly level, he sat down to rest and wait for Izzy.

He sat panting for a moment and looked around. A glass leaf stood up from the rest of the leg and made a nice backrest for him to lean against. It was almost comfortable if you didn't look down. He could see where the leg met the tabletop not far ahead. At that point, it dipped completely under the glass top and formed a fancy curve. But they could scramble up onto the tabletop before that.

Soon Isabelle joined him and sat down, panting. "That was a lot less fun than it seemed from the floor."

"I don't know," he said, "it didn't really look like fun from down there either." He looked at the glass tabletop. "I'm not sure you'll need a boost to get on."

"It was hard to tell from the bottom," she said. "We better get going."

Carter stood and followed the mildly slanted table leg. As it came closer to the point where it dipped under the table, the walkway grew narrower and narrower. Finally, it was too thin for safety and they were still several feet from the tabletop.

"I'm going to have to jump," he called back to Isabelle.

"I can't jump that far," she said and, for the first time, she sounded a little scared.

"You don't have to. I can get the key. Just back up a little so I can get a running start." He heard her backing up along the slanted table leg. He backed up as well, until he was sure he had several body lengths ahead of him before the jump.

"Just remember," he whispered to himself, "it's just a suit."

Then, with a yell, he ran along the last stretch of table leg and jumped. For a moment, it seemed as if he hung in space, incredibly far above the floor. Then his feet slammed into the tabletop and he rolled forward.

"I made it," he yelled.

He stood and looked around, spotting the key in the middle of the huge, flat glass surface. Before hurrying toward it, he looked down through the glass and saw his cousin's anxious face below him. The textured glass gave her an odd alien look.

"Brings out the real you," he muttered.

The communication between suits must have carried his remark clearly because she made a face at him. "Just get the key," he heard in his ear. She was back to being his bossy cousin.

It wasn't long before he stood back over her, waving the key at her. It was a big key, nearly half the length of his arm.

"You can't climb with that thing," she yelled.

"I'm going to throw it off the edge," he yelled back. "We can collect it at the bottom." He walked to the edge of the table and pitched it off. As he looked down, he realized that getting down might be harder than getting up. Jumping back down to the curving table leg required absolutely perfect aim. If he missed or even wobbled, he would find out just how much pain these suits could inflict.

He saw his cousin looking anxiously at him across the gap. "Are you going to jump?" she asked.

"Do you see another choice?"

She shook her head.

Carter took a few deep breaths and reminded himself again that they weren't really as high in the air as they seemed. He was pretty sure that didn't make him feel a bit better, but he thought it was worth a try.

He stepped back a few feet, but not enough to make it hard to keep his eye on the perfect landing spot. He took a deep breath and ran. Then he jumped.

In that instant, he knew his angle was wrong. He would hit the leg but not squarely. He wasn't likely to be able to stay on the slick surface. He lunged toward center and landed face down before sliding toward the edge.

Something grabbed the back of his shirt, halting his slide. He scrambled back up onto the leg. His cousin let go of his shirt as he sat up. "Thanks, Isabelle," he said.

She didn't answer but managed a weak smile. He wondered if his face looked as pale as hers.

"You know, adventures seem more fun when you just talk about them," Carter said.

Isabelle nodded. They rested a moment, then they began the slow climb back down the table leg.

Since Carter had discovered looking down was a really bad idea, he had to feel for every foothold before resting on it. On the way up, he'd been able to watch for the easiest ascent. Now everything had to be done by touch. Plus, it didn't help that Isabelle was the more confident climber, meaning he had to dodge her sneakered foot more than once.

When his feet finally touched the floor, Carter seriously considered kissing the ground. But he decided against it in front of his cousin. He settled for flopping down on the floor to rest.

THE QUEEN'S GARDEN

Isabelle jumped down right after him and trotted off to find the key.

"Are you going to lay around all day?" she asked, waving the key in his face.

"Your energy level is unnatural," he grumbled as he scrambled to his feet.

They headed down the hall until they came to the blue curtain. Isabelle slipped the huge key in the oversized lock and turned. The key clicked in the lock and the door slowly swung open.

Izzy held up one hand. "We're looking for a fountain. That's where the exit lies. We have to solve a puzzle and then the program will simply shut down and dump us back into the suits."

They stepped through the doorway into a beautiful garden. In the distance, Carter could hear the splashing of water and grinned. That must be the fountain and their way out. A large rose tree stood near the entrance of the garden. The roses growing on it were white, but three gardeners huddled around it, busily painting the roses red.

Carter glanced at his cousin and she smiled. "Believe it or not, this part is normal."

One of the three gardeners wore a white satin vest over a bright white shirt, now speckled with drops of red paint. Carter realized that two red hearts were stitched onto each sleeve near the shoulder. The man glared at the gardener who stood closest to him.

"Look out now, Five! Don't go splashing paint over me like that!" Two said.

"I couldn't help it. Seven jogged my elbow," said Five, in a sulky tone. Carter looked closely at the man and saw his sleeves had five hearts stitched on them. He wondered if that signified their rank or their names. Five gestured toward the third gardener with his dripping brush, flinging several more drops of paint on himself and the other man.

This third gardener wore seven hearts on his sleeve. He looked peevishly at the drops of paint Five had splashed on him. "That's right, Five!" he snapped. "Always lay the blame on others!"

"*You'd* better not talk!" said Five as he flung more paint. "I heard the Queen say only yesterday you deserved to be beheaded!"

"What for?" asked the one who had spoken first.

"That's none of *your* business, Two!" said Seven. "I'm sure your head has come near the chopping block a time or two."

"Yes, it *is* his business!" Five insisted. By now, so much paint was flying from man to man that it seemed almost accidental when any hit the flowers. "And I'll tell him—it was for bringing the cook tulip-roots instead of onions."

Seven flung down his brush. "Well, of all the unjust things—" he began. Then he spotted Carter and Isabelle watching them. He quickly retrieved his brush and stood up stiffly. The others looked around also, and all of them bowed low.

"Would you tell me," Isabelle said, her voice sounding stiff as if she were struggling to remember the right lines, "why you are painting those roses?"

Five and Seven said nothing, but looked at Two. Two began in a low voice, "Why the fact is, you see, Miss, this here ought to have been a *red* rose tree, and we put a white one in by mistake. If the Queen were to find out, we should all have our heads cut off, you know. So you see, Miss, we're doing our best. Though we know the paint won't weather the storm. Not a bit of it. Storms roar so and they're hard on the paint."

"Storms are clever that way," Five added. "Very clever."

"Do you know the name of this storm?" Isabelle asked.

"We do, Miss," Two said. "Would you like to know?"

At this moment, Five, who had been anxiously looking across the garden, called out, "The Queen! The Queen!" The three gardeners instantly threw themselves flat upon their faces.

To Carter's amazement, the men seemed to grow flatter and flatter as they spread themselves on the ground. Soon, they looked like rectangles with hands and feet at the corners and a head on top.

There was the sound of many footsteps. Carter looked around slowly. He wasn't eager to see what weirdness the book would throw at them next. The royal procession was a lengthy one. Ten soldiers marched in with clubs on their shoulders like rifles. The soldiers weren't quite as flat as the gardeners but they still looked decidedly boxy.

So did the ten fancily dressed men and women

who came next, walking in pairs. Their white satin costumes were studded with diamonds and looked prissy and embarrassing to Carter. Then ten children skipped in holding hands and giggling at the gardeners sprawled in the dirt.

Carter was beginning to wonder how long this parade was going to last. A collection of kings and queens swept in, peering down at everyone around them from their long pointy noses. The White Rabbit hurried along with the royalty, smiling and nodding nervously whenever anyone spoke.

A guy about Carter's age followed all the kings and queens. His costume included knee-length satin pants and a white velvet coat embroidered with hearts. He carried a red velvet cushion with a crown perched on it. Carter felt bad for the poor guy and stepped forward to start a conversation, but Izzy pulled him back.

"Low profile," she whispered. "Once they get past, we can head for the fountain."

The White Rabbit stepped up beside Carter

and blew a trumpet practically in his ear. Carter jumped back and shook his head.

"Are you crazy?" he snapped.

The rabbit simply ignored him and shouted. "Their royal highnesses, the King and Queen of Hearts!"

The Queen of Hearts stepped close to Izzy and peered down at her for a long moment. Then she turned to her husband and said, "Who is this?"

"I'm certain I don't know, my dearest heart of storm," the thin man said timidly. "She is only a child."

The queen glared at him and turned to the young man with the cushion. "Jack?"

The young man cast a bored look at Alice, then started to shrug. The queen's frown intensified, so he bowed and smiled instead. The queen's face grew nearly as red as the hearts on her gown. She glared at Izzy, "Who are you?"

Izzy did her best imitation of a curtsy and Carter snickered. "My name is Isabelle, so please

Your Majesty."

Carter's laugh drew the angry woman's attention. "And who is that!"

"My cousin, Your Highness," Izzy said. "He means no harm, Majesty. He's a bit witless."

The queen's eyes narrowed as she studied Carter silently, then she turned back to Isabelle. "Do you play croquet?"

"I can, Highness," Isabelle said carefully. "But my cousin and I are due . . ."

"He plays croquet, too?" the queen asked, turning her sharp glance toward Carter again. "He looks in need of a good lightning bolt, but he may come along."

The queen grabbed Isabelle's arm and began towing her along to a lush, grassy field that was full of ridges and furrows. Hedgehogs ambled around the grass and tall flamingos stood in a bunch—each perched on one leg with its head tucked under a wing.

Finally the queen let go of Izzy's arm and shouted, "Get to your places."

People rushed around the field crazily. Some bumped into one another and others tripped over the wandering hedgehogs and landed facedown on the ground. Every time someone fell, the queen would insist he or she become a croquet wicket.

In the wild disorder, Carter stepped up behind Izzy. "I remember this part," he said. "Flamingo croquet should be a blast!"

"We don't have time for that," Isabelle said. "We need to get to the fountain and get out of here."

"Sure, finally something fun and now you're ready to get me out of here," Carter grumbled. Then he perked up. "I just want to hit one ball and we can go." He trotted to the nearest clutch of sleeping flamingos and grabbed one, causing a flurry of flapping and wiggling. It wasn't easy to get the head pointing down while holding the body still. Carter finally managed to stuff the body under one arm with its legs hanging down slightly behind him.

Then he stalked over to a rolled-up hedgehog to give it a whack. He carefully straightened out the flamingo's neck and aimed at the hedgehog. Suddenly, the flamingo twisted itself around and peered up into Carter's face with its tiny blinking eyes. Nose to nose with the flamingo, Carter burst into laughter.

"Come on," Izzy snapped. She had stalked over and poked him.

The flamingo took one look at the glaring girl and tried to tuck its head back under its wing. But since the body was stuffed under Carter's arm, it only managed to slam its long beak into his stomach a few times, making him laugh and gasp at the same time.

Carter backed away and looked for his hedgehog. He spotted it scurrying away with another escaped croquet ball.

"Okay, I give up," he said, setting the flamingo gently on the ground. It hurried off to join its friends. "Let's go."

Carter and Isabelle were headed back to the

rose garden when they heard the shriek of the queen behind them. "Where are you going?" she yelled.

They turned to find the queen pointing at them. "I did not give you permission to leave!" she screamed.

"We are very late," Izzy said.

"Off with her head!" the queen shouted.

THE FOUNTAIN

"Come on," Carter said, grabbing Izzy's hand and running for the rose garden. A group of soldiers popped up in front of them almost magically. Carter dropped Izzy's hand and rushed at the soldiers. They flailed away at him with the clubs, but they had grown flat and rectangular like the gardeners. With their hands at the top corners of their boxy bodies, they couldn't seem to get much force behind the blows. Still, "Ouch!" Carter yelled as he grabbed one of the clubs and threw it as far as he could over the heads of the soldiers.

Another club whacked him on the side of the head. This time, Carter wrenched it away and used it to knock down the whole row of soldiers. They fell like dominos and lay on the ground kicking their feet and waving their hands.

"Come on, Izzy," Carter called. He spun around and sprinted through the bit of low hedge that separated the croquet fields from the rose garden. Isabelle raced along behind him, but just as she passed the gap in the hedge, a huge head burst out of the bushes. It looked like an eagle head and it snapped at Isabelle, catching hold of her by the back of her dress.

"Hey, let her go!" Carter yelled.

The creature stepped the rest of way out of the bushes with Izzy dangling from its beak. It definitely wasn't an eagle, though it had huge wings and its chest was covered with feathers. This creature had four legs. The front two looked like eagle talons but the back end of the creature looked like a huge lion with a lion's tail and lion legs. It was a griffin.

"Oh, come on," Carter said as he looked around for a weapon to use against the huge creature. "This is supposed to be a kids' book!"

"Put me down!" Izzy shouted, wiggling and kicking.

Carter spotted one of the soldier's discarded clubs and grabbed it. He swung as hard as he could and smacked the griffin's neck. The club shattered to dust and the griffin turned to slap Carter with his tail, knocking him back into the bushes.

"Hey, leave Carter alone," Isabelle yelled. "And put me down, right now!"

"Uh cand," the griffon said, its voice muffled from having a mouthful of Izzy. "Ee had do go shee da bock turble."

"What's it want?" Carter said, scrambling out of the bush.

"I think it's saying we have to go see the mock turtle," Isabelle said as the griffin stretched its long wings a few times. "That's the next thing Alice does after the croquet match. Look, I don't think we can get it to put me down. You go to the fountain and solve the riddle. It should dump us both out at the same time when it shuts down."

"Why a riddle?" Carter asked. "Why not push a button or something?"

The griffin began to flap its huge wings and the sound nearly drowned out Izzy's voice. "Because the hacker closed the program exits unless you win something," she yelled. "A puzzle seemed the fastest thing to win. You just find the answer and we're out."

"So what's the answer?" Carter yelled.

Izzy's shouted response was lost as the griffin leaped into flight, carrying Isabelle away.

"Off with his head!"

Carter heard the queen's bellow behind him, followed by the sound of running feet. He didn't even turn to look. He just ran in the direction of the splashing sounds, hoping that signaled the fountain and their escape from this crazy book. He dodged several half-painted rose bushes and jumped over one gardener, bent nearly double to reach some roses at the bottom of the bush with red paint.

Carter raced across a small stretch of bare lawn and slipped through a gap in the far hedge. He expected to see the fountain, but instead he found himself immediately facing another hedge. Passages between the hedge rows led to his right and left.

"Oh great," he groaned. "A maze. Which way should I go?"

He heard another bellow from behind him in the rose garden and decided it might not be a good idea to spend a long time choosing. He picked right and trotted along in that direction. *Technically,* he thought, *a maze is a kind of puzzle. Maybe I just need to solve the maze and reach the fountain, then we'll get home.*

At the end of the right-hand passage, he faced another hedge wall. This time the only choice was to go left, so he did. He came to a break on the left side. He now could go straight or left. He chose straight and ran until he had only one choice, a left turn. He started down the row but slowed to a stop. A statue of the

Queen of Hearts glared down at him. He'd hit a dead end.

"Well, I guess if it was easy," Carter muttered. He turned around and trotted back the way he'd come and finished, "they wouldn't call it a puzzle."

When he came to the first opening in the right side hedge, he paused. The fountain might be at the center of the maze. In that case, he should go deeper into the maze instead of running around the outside. He turned to his right and soon faced another choice to turn right or left.

Carter could see both ways ran into a wall fairly quickly, but he couldn't see whether they had any turns before hitting what looked like a dead end. He decided to go right, since it was a longer stretch before he'd run into a hedge wall. When he finally reached the far hedge, the only way to go was another right. He saw another ugly statue of the queen at the end of that row.

"Izzy!" he yelled. "If you designed this maze,

I hope that stupid griffin eats you."

He turned around and ran straight down the hedge row, passing the opening on his left and staying straight until he hit another wall. The hedge corridor turned left and then a sharp right followed by another left. But Carter didn't see any ugly statues, so he continued on.

He came to an opening on his right but he could see the Queen statue glaring at him without going down that path. Then ahead, he spotted another statue. He slowed down, feeling a flash of frustration. Surely there was an answer to this maze. That's when he spotted a break in the hedge, not far from the statue alcove.

He turned right into the break and then another left. He hurried forward until he came to a small, open area with a stone bench. Two openings led off the clearing, one straight ahead of him and one off to the right. He decided to go right.

He went only a short way before the maze

turned to the right again and opened out into a large, grassy square. In the center stood a round, dry fountain. He'd made it! He walked closer to the fountain, waiting for the program to go dark. Nothing happened.

Carter moaned. The maze must not have been the puzzle. That meant he still had more to go.

He looked over the fountain. The base was a round marble pool, about the size of a backyard kiddie pool. In the center of that pool was a pedestal with a smaller round pool on it. And in the center of that was another pedestal. This one had a statue. The marble statue looked exactly like Isabelle holding a pitcher as if ready to pour water into the fountain.

"Stuck on yourself much?" he groaned, looking over the figure.

Suddenly, Carter heard a rustling behind him. He turned and spotted two of the gardeners carrying watering cans. They rushed over to the fountain.

"I need water," one of the gardeners shouted.

"What do you have for me?" the marble statue of Isabelle asked in a gravelly voice.

"Um," the gardener looked around in a panic. He grabbed a rock from the ground and held it up. "A rock?"

"No!" the statue shrieked and the rock tumbled from the terrified gardener's hand. The stone statue turned the pitcher toward him and water blasted from it like a fire hose. It knocked the gardener head over heels. The statue then turned its marble head with a rough grinding sound and stared at the second gardener. "What do you have for me?"

The gardener trembled, his eyes huge. He looked around but all he could see was the same rock.

"What do you have for me?" the statue demanded.

The gardener grabbed the rock from the ground and held it out. He was shaking so much that the weight of the rock in his outstretched

90

arm nearly tipped him over. "This s-s-s-stone?"

The statue smiled. "Thank you. You win."

Water flowed gently from the tilted pitcher into the fountain and the two gardeners quickly filled their watering cans and ran for the exit. They nearly knocked each other down as they squeezed through the gap in the hedge at the same time.

"What kind of puzzle is that?" Carter asked. "You don't want the rock one minute and then you do want it the next."

The statue turned to look at him. The grinding sound of marble on marble made his teeth ache. The sculpture stared at him, its blank white eyes fastened on him. "What do you have for me?

Carter frowned in concentration. What did he have to give the fountain?

ESCAPE FROM WONDERLAND

Carter picked up the same rock the gardeners had offered. "A rock?" he said hopefully.

"No!" shrieked the marble Isabelle. The blast of water from the pitcher hit Carter in the stomach, knocking him back onto the same wet patch of ground where the gardener had fallen before him. The water continued to rain down on him until he was completely soaked.

"Enough already!" he yelled, holding up a hand. "Can I give you something else?" The statue merely turned away and looked back toward the gap in the hedge. He stood up and walked around until the statue was facing him again. But the statue's gaze passed over his head. It refused to look at him again.

"Do you want this rock?" he asked. He bent his knees slightly so he could jump away if the statue tried to blast him again. He carefully held out the same rock again, but the statue never moved. "Don't you want this rock?"

Nothing. He might as well have been talking to a statue.

Carter sighed and slumped down on the side of the fountain, his clothes dripping into the stone basin. Apparently he couldn't just offer the same thing twice. It wouldn't even acknowledge him now. So the puzzle must have another answer.

Suddenly he wondered if it were capable of knowing it was him if he left the small clearing and came back. He hopped up and headed back out into the maze. Then he walked back up to the fountain.

Again, he heard the grinding sound of the statue moving. "What do you have for me?"

Carter grinned, sure he knew the answer

now. He grabbed the rock and held it out. "A rock?"

"No!" the marble Isabelle shrieked and the water knocked him on his rear again.

"Oh, come on," Carter yelled back, sputtering as the water rained down on him. "You took it from the gardener!"

He flopped backward into the puddle, not caring about the mud and water soaking into his clothes. He was tired, he was hungry, and he had no idea how to solve the puzzle. Why did the fountain take the rock when the second gardener offered it?

Then, he heard scurrying from the hedge. Another gardener popped around the edge. He hurried up to the fountain.

"What do you have for me?" the fountain asked fiercely.

The gardener shifted from foot to foot nervously, scratching his head while he thought. Then he reached down and pulled off his shoe. "This shoe?"

The marble Isabelle smiled, a creepy look with the dead, flat, white eyes. "Thank you. You win."

Water flowed smoothly into the fountain basins and the gardener cheerfully filled his watering can and hurried back out the maze.

Carter sat up straight. A shoe works? He hesitated. Maybe not, considering the rock only worked for one gardener. He wasn't in a big hurry for another soaking. Maybe he'd wait and see if another example might come along.

Sure enough, another pair of gardeners poked their heads into the clearing and then hurried in. The first of the pair offered his watering can and was blasted halfway across the lawn. The second offered a stocking. The statue smiled and filled the fountain again. When the gardeners left, Carter thought about what the offerings had in common.

"Okay, you don't like the watering can and sometimes you don't like the rock," he said, frowning as he worked out the puzzle. "But you did like a shoe and a stocking."

Suddenly his memory and the answer hit him. The fountain didn't like the rock. It only liked it when the gardener called it a "stone." It liked shoe, stocking, and stone but not rock or watering can. Grinning, Carter stood and headed back out of the clearing. He snapped a bit of dead branch from one of the hedges close to him. Then he took a deep breath and strode back into the clearing.

The stone Isabelle glared down at him. "What do you have for me?"

He held up the piece of branch. "A stick!"

"Thank you," the statue said with its icy smile. "You win!"

Carter cheered as pitch darkness slammed down on him. "Game over!" he yelled.

Carter sensed the virtual reality suit around him, even though he couldn't see anything at all. He leaned backward and felt the back of the suit give, allowing him to wriggle out. Water sloshed out with him. The story might have been virtual, but it was clear the suit had soaked his clothes.

"You made that hard enough, Izzy," he snapped as he stepped out into the small room. A drizzle of icy water dripped from his hair and ran down the back of his shirt.

It felt weird to be back in his uncle's basement after spending so long in Wonderland. He looked around, expecting to see Isabelle standing next to her own suit, smirking at his wet clothes and how long it had taken him to figure out the puzzle. She wasn't in the room.

Then he saw the other suit move, raising an arm and lifting one foot and then the other. Because the suit hung in the air, the feet never touched the floor, but each step gave the perfect illusion of Isabelle walking on an invisible surface. She was still inside experiencing some kind of virtual reality.

"What are you doing in there?" Carter asked as he walked over to her suit, leaving a small puddle with each step. "Come on, Izzy. I'm wet,

I'm hungry, and I could really use a bathroom break." He pulled at the seam in the back of the suit, but it was sealed tightly shut.

The suit continued to move. Isabelle wasn't just flailing around in the dark inside the suit, she was walking forward as if she were going somewhere. She clearly was still living inside the book. Solving the puzzle had shut down the program for Carter, but not for Isabelle.

He walked around to the front of the suit's helmet. "Isabelle!" he yelled. "Can you hear me? Isabelle!" Isabelle simply kept walking in the suit, bringing one foot forward and slamming it into Carter's knee. He jumped back and fell on his rear again, his sodden jeans hitting the thin carpet with a sploosh. "Watch it. I'm going to have bruises as it is."

Carter looked at the suit helplessly. How was he supposed to get Isabelle out? He wasn't the computer genius. He was just the guy who dropped cell phones in the toilet.

EXTRACTING ALICE

Carter wrenched open the door to the small basement room and ran out to the computer station. He stared at the code on the screen, wiping a clump of dripping hair back away from his forehead.

The moving code didn't mean a thing to him, but it was still scrolling so he assumed the program was still running. Then, very faintly, he heard Izzy's voice as if she were speaking from a great distance or talking with a bag over her head. He went back to the suit room, "Izzy?" he yelled.

He couldn't hear the voice in there at all, so he turned to slosh back to the table. "Izzy?" he yelled again.

Very faintly, he heard, "Carter?"

Where was her voice coming from? Carter looked at the scattered piles on the desk. His uncle's log lay open on the table but it didn't lay flat. Something was underneath. Carter moved the log over to the next table and saw it had been laying on a headphones and microphone combination.

"Bingo!" he said. He pulled his shirt over his head and used it to wipe his face and hair so he didn't electrocute himself when he put on the headphones. The shirt was already wet, so it only helped slightly. Still he hoped for the best and slipped the headphones on. "Izzy?"

"Carter!" she yelled. "Where are you?"

"I'm out of the suit. The book shut down for me. Thanks for the soaking, by the way," he said. "Where are you?"

"I'm listening to a griffin and a mock turtle argue about a lobster's dance."

"Why didn't the program let you out when it dumped me?" Carter's voice rose.

Izzy didn't answer. "Izzy?"

"Let me think," she said, then snapped. "No, I won't join the dance!"

Carter suppressed a snicker. It was nice to have someone else dealing with the bizarre Wonderland. He tapped his fingers on the desk, waiting for Isabelle to decide what he should do.

Suddenly he had an idea. "What if I just cut the power?" His finger inched toward the master switch on his uncle's main surge protector.

"No!" she yelped. "If you cut the power, it would shut down the suit completely."

"Don't we want that?"

"I don't think so," she said. "If I had to take a wild guess, I'd say all the air in the suit gets pumped in. If you shut off the power, the suit won't release *and* it won't cycle air. I would rather not hang in the dark holding my breath."

"Oh, okay," Carter flopped in the swivel chair in front of the bank of computer monitors. "Then we still don't know how to get you out."

"I think the reason it didn't shut down and let me out is because I'm not functioning as a visitor in the program," she said. "I took over Alice, and since I'm still doing things, the computer can't shut down the program because I'm holding it open somehow."

"So maybe you just have to go through the book to the end," Carter said. "How much is left after this lobster dance part?"

"Well, first the turtle sings really, really badly," Isabelle said.

"How do you know he sings badly?"

"He's doing it now. Anyway, I think the trial is after that. Then the queen tries to have Alice's head cut off and all the playing cards attack."

"That doesn't sound good," Carter said.

"Not really, but then Alice wakes up and that realistically should let me out of the program."

"If the book acts normal, whatever normal is for this book," Carter said. "But when I was in the book, the March Hare tried to chew my head off with steel teeth. So I'm not sure it's safe for you to stay in there."

"Well, if you have another idea, I'm open to it," Izzy said. "Until then, the griffin is taking me to the trial. On the up side, the turtle stopped singing."

"What if we put in another exit," Carter said. "One you could use as a character."

"You want to mess with the computer code?" Izzy's voice came out high and weird. "Have you lost your mind?"

"I can type," Carter said. "I get great scores in keyboarding. If you tell me what to put in, I can type it. You're supposed to be the super brain computer geek, tell me what to type and I'll put it in."

"I'm a little distracted here," she said. In the background, Carter heard someone shouting, "Silence in the court!" Then he heard some mumbling and three trumpet blasts.

"Everything looks okay so far," Izzy said. "Maybe we can just wait it out."

Carter listened as a distant voice read the

crime: "The Queen of Hearts, she made some tarts, all on a summer day. A summer storm blew them all home, and killed them dead that day!"

"Uh oh," Izzy said.

"That does not sound normal," Carter said.

He heard someone bellow through the headphones. "Who dares speak at the trial? Bring her here!"

Carter heard the sound of a scuffle, then a strange flat voice that said, "You're not Alice, I can tell. You don't have her eyes and you don't have her smell."

"You are one creepy bunny," Izzy said.

"Come and face the storm, Mock Alice," the White Rabbit said.

"Okay, Carter," Isabelle said breathlessly over the sound of more scuffle, "I guess you're the programmer. Do you see the screen where the code is scrolling? The keyboard in front of it will let you jump ahead. Click on page down. Watch for—"

Suddenly Isabelle's voice stopped. The background sounds vanished and all Carter heard was dead air in his ears.

"Hey!" he yelled. "You told me to push page down! Why did you tell me that if it was going to break everything!"

He stared at the screen in front of him. The code had stopped scrolling when he hit the page down key. Now it was just static lines of gibberish as far as he was concerned.

Then a box popped up on the screen. It looked a little like an instant message screen but no usernames were defined. As he watched, keystrokes appeared on the screen in the box:

"Having fun yet?"

The line sat unmoving on the screen. Carter leaned forward slowly and typed.

"Who R U?"

"U guess"

Someone wanted to play games. Carter thought about who had been playing games with them all along. He took a deep breath and typed, "U hacked R program."

"X-cellent. Did U guess my name?"

Carter gritted his teeth. The guy had Izzy trapped in a suit with who knows what happening and he still wants to play guessing games. Carter practically pounded the next response. "How do I shut down the program?"

"Did U guess my name?

"4-get it. How do I shut down the program?"

"Did U guess my name?"

Carter flopped backward into the computer chair. The hacker wasn't going to say anything until Carter guessed the name. He thought about all the clues they'd seen. The first one about cats and thunder feet and the book with the wrong title, something about a tornado. Then the weird animals got glassy eyed about the weather when he was in Wonderland. At the tea party, they starting talking about a storm before the March Hare grew steel teeth and now the White Rabbit was saying something about a storm to Isabelle before she was cut off.

So some kind of weather talk preceded every bit of weirdness.

"Okay, weather," Carter muttered. "Weatherman? Rainmaker?" He leaned over and typed: "How many guesses do I get?"

"One. But I will give you a hint, Moist Arm. Good luck."

The window vanished from the screen and Carter was back to watching code scroll. He moaned and grabbed a sheet of paper from the table to write down the clue. What could *moist arm* mean? If you stood out in the rain, you'd get a moist arm. Maybe the hacker was rain man or rainmaker.

He stared at the paper. Maybe it was more of a puzzle then a clue. He thought of puzzles that had clues like that. "It could be a hinky pinky," he said. "Like moist puppy could be wet pet or soggy doggy."

He wrote down all the words he could think of that meant moist: soggy, wet, damp, drippy, soaked. No matter how many he wrote, he couldn't think of any matching rhyme that meant arm. In fact, the only arm synonym he could come up with was limb.

"Plus, none of this has anything to do with all the weather stuff," Carter said, crumpling up the paper in his frustration. "This isn't getting Izzy out."

Carter smoothed the paper back out and stared at the words. "Think," he murmured. "What other kind of puzzle could this be?"

He wondered if it had to do with the number of letters. There were eight letters. "What if I put them in alphabetical order?" He bent over the paper and sang the alphabet song in his head as he rewrote the letters: a i m m o r s t. "Aim morst? Not helpful." Then as he stared at it, the word "morst" leaped out at him. "Storm! Morst anagrams to storm!"

Storm definitely fit all the weather stuff. But what about "aim." Was he supposed to aim the storm at something. "Aim, mia, iam," he said, then grinned. "I am. I am storm!"

Carter whooped and leaned over the keyboard to type *Storm*. He held his breath, then hit "enter." The screen went blank. For an instant, Carter felt a surge of panic. Had he saved the day or messed up everything? He remembered what Izzy had said about the amount of air in the suits and dashed for the small room.

Isabelle was wriggling out of the backside of her bulky suit like a really annoyed caterpillar breaking out of a cocoon. "That took you long enough," she snapped.

"Excuse me?" he said. "You definitely left me in there way longer than I left you."

Isabelle nodded. "The queen was getting a little too eager to see my head whacked off," she said as she rubbed her neck. "I have a whole new respect for bunnies now that I've seen one with an axe."

Carter flashed back to the March Hare and his sharp steel teeth. "I know what you mean." Then he perked up. "I also know the hacker's name. I had to enter it into the program to get the book to shut down."

"Hey, that's pretty smart," she said. "How did you know to try that?"

Carter explained about his little chat with the hacker.

"That guy sure likes games," Isabelle said. "And it's clear that he doesn't have any problem with Uncle Dan's security."

"I know something else that's clear," Carter said, crossing his arms. "No amount of money is going to get me back in one of those suits."

Isabelle laughed. "That doesn't sound like my action-hero cousin."

Both cousins jumped as a phone began ringing. They tracked the sound down to a table covered with papers. Rooting around, Carter unearthed the phone. The caller ID showed Uncle Dan was calling. He turned the call to speakerphone. "Uncle Dan," he said, "the hacker is named Storm."

"Oh no," Uncle Dan said. "I was afraid of that. Okay, I'll get some people on it. And I have some ideas for how you can patch the holes there, Isabelle. But I'll send you instructions through a more secure avenue."

"You're not coming home?" Izzy asked.

"Soon, but not yet. Don't worry, though, I have a few more jobs for you guys." Then their uncle's voice turned eager. "So now that you've spent some time with everything, did you have fun?"

Izzy and Carter looked at one another and burst out laughing. Finally, Carter calmed down enough to gasp, "Sure, it was killer."

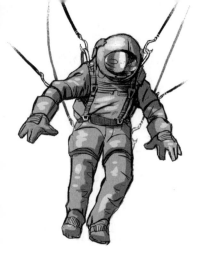

Now that they know the name of the hacker, it is up to Carter, Izzy, and Uncle Dan to track Storm down and save their virtual reality suits!

Follow the adventure in

Book 2
The Calm Before the Storm
A Night in Sleepy Hollow